This book belongs to

_____

Published by Scholastic Inc., 90 Old Sherman Turnpike, Danbury, Connecticut 06816.

ISBN: 0-7172-9955-4

Printed in the U.S.A.

First Scholastic printing, June 2006

Hats Off to Lyle

A Lesson in Forgiveness

by **Ronald Kidd**

Illustrated by **Tom Bancroft** and **Rob Corley**

Colored by **Jon Conkling**

SCHOLASTIC INC.

New York Toronto London Auckland Sydney
Mexico City New Delhi Hong Kong Buenos Aires

You've probably heard all about Vikings—you know, those rough guys with funny-looking hats. It's true, they sailed the seas, pillaging and plundering.

There was one group of Vikings, though, who sailed the seas; and instead of pillaging, they were quite pleasant. Instead of causing trouble, they did **nice** things for people.

They were rather strange—but in a good way.

Across the lake from the nice Vikings lived a group of mean, stinky Vikings. They went around breaking, burning, and smashing other people's things. They didn't even brush their teeth!

And when they thought about those nice Vikings, the stinky Vikings got really angry!

"Those nice Vikings are making us look bad," said Ugalee, the leader of the stinky Vikings.

His men replied, "We already look bad. Have you seen your hair lately?"

Of all the nice Vikings, the nicest was a young asparagus named Lyle.

He didn't sail much. Lyle preferred to stay home, knitting and making crafts,

such as hat covers. He was really good at it.

But when Lyle told his friends about knitting hat covers, Olaf, their leader, was confused. "A hat needs a cover?" asked Olaf. "I thought a hat *was* a cover."

"Maybe so," said Lyle, "but they're really cool."

Olaf said, "If I want to be cool, I'll sit on an iceberg."

The other Vikings laughed. Lyle turned red, which isn't easy for an asparagus.

Two of the Vikings felt sorry for Lyle. Their names were Ottar and Sven.

"You know," said Ottar, "you really should come sailing with us. We row, we sweat, and we sing a little karaoke . . ."

Lyle said, "Thanks, but I need to work on these hat covers."

"Why don't you bring them along?" Sven said. "I'm sure the guys won't mind."

Sven was right—sort of. When Lyle arrived at the ship with his knitting stuff, the guys didn't mind—laughing their heads off, that is.

As they sailed on, the whole crew laughed louder and louder.

"Hey, Lyle, I have a hole in my sock. Can you fix it?" asked one Viking.

Another Viking pointed to Lyle's knitting needle. "Your spear's kind of small, isn't it?" he teased.

Lyle just kept knitting. He wasn't having much fun, but he sure made a lot of hat covers.

Before long, the ship landed at a monastery,
where a group of monks lived.

"Vikings!" the monks yelled.

"Hide the good china!"

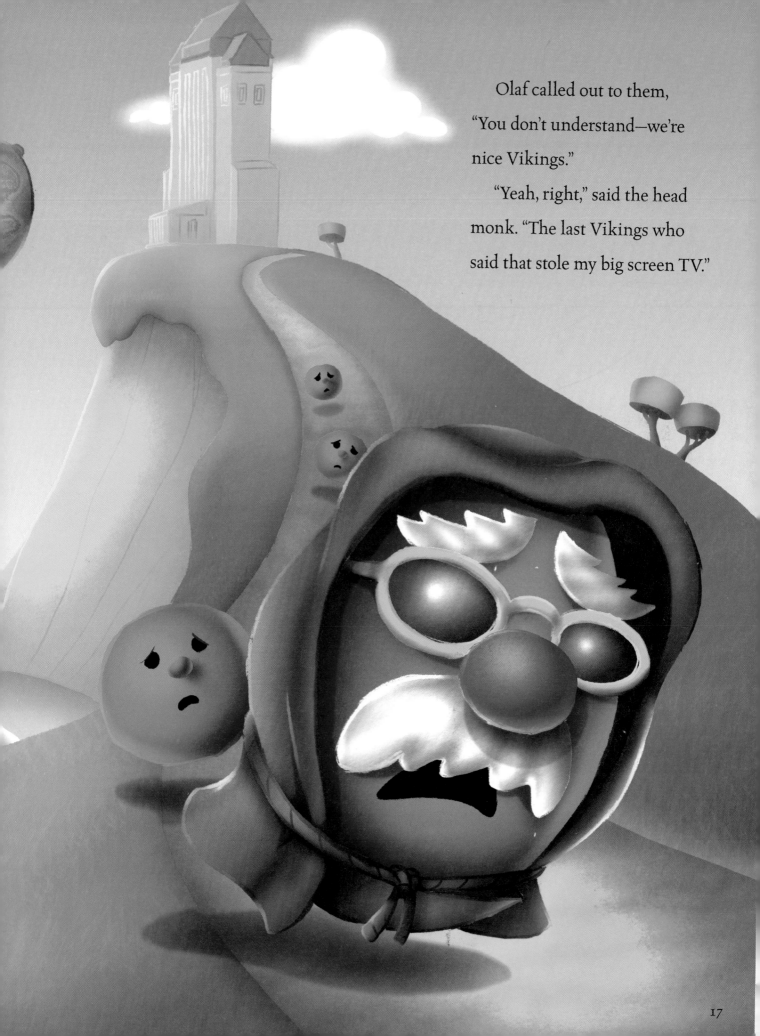

Olaf called out to them, "You don't understand—we're nice Vikings."

"Yeah, right," said the head monk. "The last Vikings who said that stole my big screen TV."

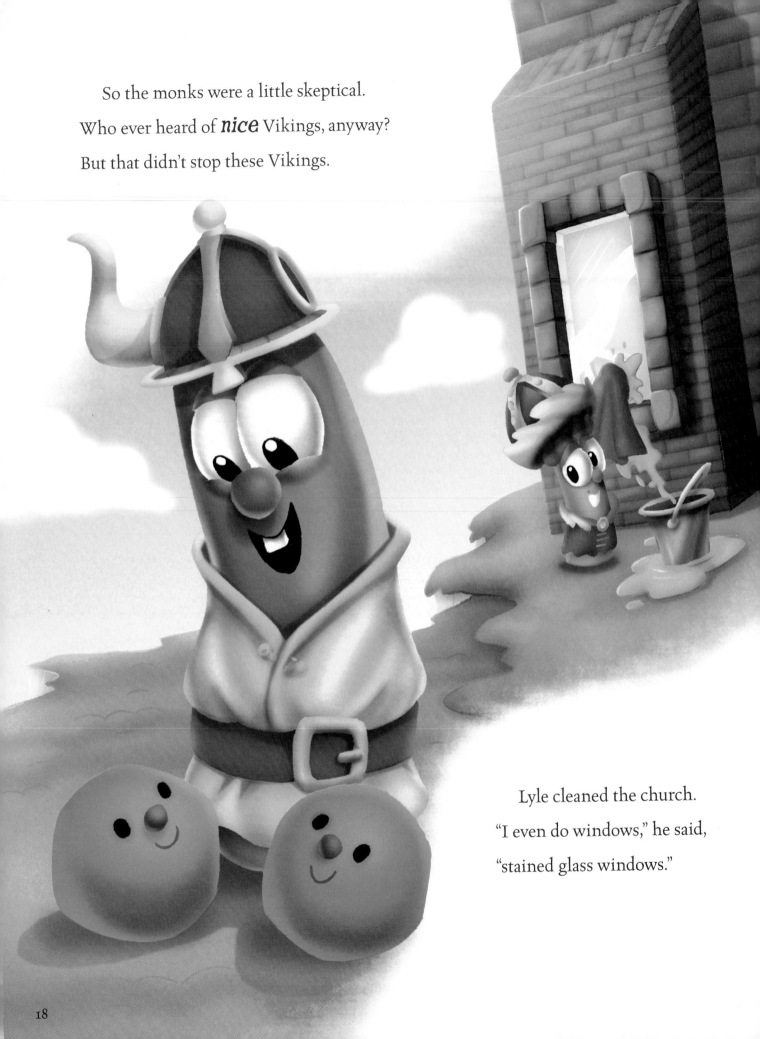

So the monks were a little skeptical.

Who ever heard of *nice* Vikings, anyway?

But that didn't stop these Vikings.

Lyle cleaned the church.

"I even do windows," he said,

"stained glass windows."

Sven and Ottar worked in the soup kitchen. Well, it wasn't really a soup kitchen. "Hope you brought an extra pair of socks!" Sven warned and chuckled as he cooked up his famous knock-your-socks-off peanut-butter chili.

"Hey," said one monk, "you guys really are nice. You can come visit us anytime!"

While the nice Vikings were doing very good things, the stinky Vikings were doing very bad things. They had followed the nice Vikings all the way to the monastery. As soon as Lyle and the others left the ship, the stinky Vikings climbed on board. They broke the mainmast and stole the oars.

"**This** is what Vikings are supposed to do," said Ugalee as he ripped a big hole in the ship's sail.

The nice Vikings got back
just in time to see them leave.
Sven sputtered, "Those
mean, stinky Vikings.
They . . . they . . ."
"They stink,"
finished Ottar.

All day, the nice Vikings had been doing things for others. They were

really tired. It didn't seem fair that now they had to clean up their own ship.

But they did. As Olaf stepped back to look at their work, he said,

"It looks great, guys, but there's still a big problem."

"What's that?" asked Sven.

"The mast is repaired, but the oars are gone. And the sail has a huge hole in it—we aren't going anywhere!" Olaf shouted.

"Does that mean we won't make it back in time for dinner?" Sven whined. "Tonight's hamburger noodely-o night!"

Lyle studied the sail. He thought for a moment. Then he said, "If you lower the sail, there may be something I can do."

The crew brought down the sail. Lyle picked up a needle and yarn and started to sew. A few minutes later, he stepped back.

"Hey," said one of the Vikings, "the hole is gone! We can sail again!"

Olaf and the others gathered around Lyle. "We're supposed to be nice Vikings," Ottar said to Lyle. "But we haven't been very nice to you."

Sven said, "We're sorry, Lyle. Will you ever forgive us?"

"It's true that you weren't very nice," said Lyle. "But I forgive you."

The Vikings cheered.

"Thanks, Lyle," Olaf said. "Now, there's just one more thing."

"What's that?" asked Lyle.

Olaf added, "Can I have a hat cover? They're **SO** cool."

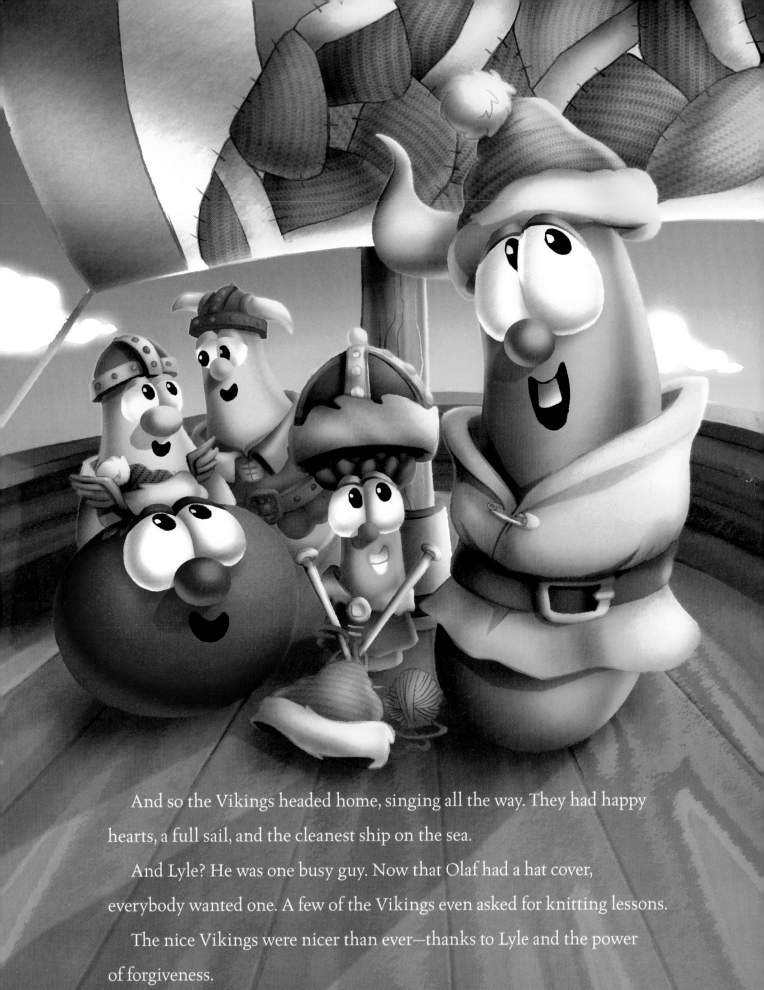

And so the Vikings headed home, singing all the way. They had happy hearts, a full sail, and the cleanest ship on the sea.

And Lyle? He was one busy guy. Now that Olaf had a hat cover, everybody wanted one. A few of the Vikings even asked for knitting lessons.

The nice Vikings were nicer than ever—thanks to Lyle and the power of forgiveness.

Put up with each other.
Forgive the things you are
holding against one another.
Forgive, just as the Lord forgave you.
Colossians 3:13